Hot Rod Hamster

AND THE WACKY WHATEVER RACE!

By **Cynthia Lord**

Cover illustration by **Derek Anderson**

Interior illustrations by **Greg Paprocki**

Scholastic Press • New York

To my teacher Mrs. Keitt, who taught me to love reading. — C. L.

For Grace, Marijka, and our entire racing team at Scholastic. — D. A.

Text copyright © 2014 by Cynthia Lord
Illustrations copyright © 2014 by Derek Anderson

LIBRARY OF CONGRESS CATALOGING-IN-PUBLICATION DATA
Lord, Cynthia, author.
Hot Rod Hamster and the Wacky Whatever Race! / by Cynthia Lord ; pictures based on the artwork of Derek Anderson ; interior illustrations by Greg Paprocki . — First edition.   pages cm
Summary: Hot Rod Hamster enlists the help of his friend Dog to build a super sleek soap box racer for the Wacky Whatever Race.
ISBN 978-0-545-69442-1 (hardcover : alk. paper) — ISBN 978-0-545-62678-1 (pbk. : alk. paper)
1. Hamsters—Juvenile fiction. 2. Coaster cars—Juvenile fiction. 3. Racing—Juvenile fiction.
4. Friendship—Juvenile fiction. [1. Hamsters—Fiction. 2. Coaster cars—Fiction. 3. Racing—Fiction.
4. Friendship—Fiction.] I. Anderson, Derek, 1969- illustrator. II. Paprocki, Greg, illustrator.
III. Title. PZ7.L87734Hov 2014 813.6—dc23 2013046940

10 9 8 7 6 5 4 3 2 1   14 15 16 17 18

Printed in Malaysia   108
First edition, September 2014

The display type was set in Ziggy ITC and Coop Black.
The text was set in Cochin Medium and Gill Sans Bold.
The interior art was created digitally by Greg Paprocki.
Art direction and book design by Marijka Kostiw

Hot Rod Hamster was on his way to the junkyard to see his friend Dog.

But as he passed the auto shop, something made him stop.

Sparky's Auto Shop

— THE —
WACKY
WHATEVER
Race

Build a superfast car to race down the hill.

Good Fun!   *Great Prizes!*

Sign up inside.

New Brakes

Oil Changes

RULES FOR THE
WACKY
WHATEVER
Race

1. The car must be made from a box.
2. It must have four wheels.
3. No motors are allowed. Each car will get only one push at the starting line to help it roll down the hill.
4. During the race, the driver's paws cannot touch the ground. Only the car's wheels can touch the ground.
5. The first car to roll across the finish line will be the winner.

Look, Dog!
This race would be
super fun for me!
This does look fun,
but your hot rod doesn't
follow the rules for this race.
Your hot rod was not made
from a box, and it has
a motor.
You're right.
I'll need a new car for
the Wacky Whatever
Race — a car that rolls
superfast!
RULES FOR THE
WACKY
WHATEVER
Race

The first thing you'll need is a box.

Big box.

Small box.

Long box.

Tall box.

Which would *you* choose?

Dog finds some tools,
and Hamster cuts a door.
Mice tape and glue.
Be careful where you pour!

Fat wheels.

Slow wheels.

Which would *you* choose?

Dog finds wheel rods,
and Hamster drills a hole.
Mice bring the wheels.
One is on a roll!

Hot flames.   Cold flames.

Pink flames.   Gold flames.

Which would *you* choose?

Dog brings some paint,
and Hamster opens cans.
Mice stir and mix.
Lots of pretty pans!

Remember to keep your helmet on. Watch out for the other cars. And don't let your paws touch the ground.

Dog gives a push, and . . .

. . . Hamster's in the lead!

Mice gasp and groan.
Hamster's losing speed!

Dog points and shouts.
Cars are coming fast!
Mice hide their eyes.
Hamster will be last.

As soon as Hot Rod Hamster's paws touch the ground, he will be out of the race.

Dog shakes his head.
Poor Hamster really tried.

Mice stare and gasp
as Hamster climbs inside!

His paws never touched the ground! Look at him go!

Dog jumps and cheers. What a perfect plan!

Can Hot Rod Hamster win the race?

Yes, of course he can!